First

published 2017

by Walker Books

Ltd, 87 Vauxhall Walk,

London SE11 5HJ • This edition

published 2018 • Text © 2017 Mac

Barnett • Illustrations © 2017 Jon

Klassen • The moral rights of the author and

illustrator have been asserted. • This book has

been typeset in ITC New Clarendon • Printed in China

from the publisher. • British Library Cataloguing in Publication Data: a

catalogue record for this book is available from the British Library

ISBN 978-1-4063-7836-8 • www.walker.co.uk • 10 9 8 7 6 5 4 3

TRIANGLE

by

Mac Barnett

&

Jon Klassen

WALKER BOOKS
AND SUBSIDIARIES
LONDON • BOSTON • SYDNEY • AUCKLAND

This is Triangle.

This is Triangle's house.

This is Triangle in his house.

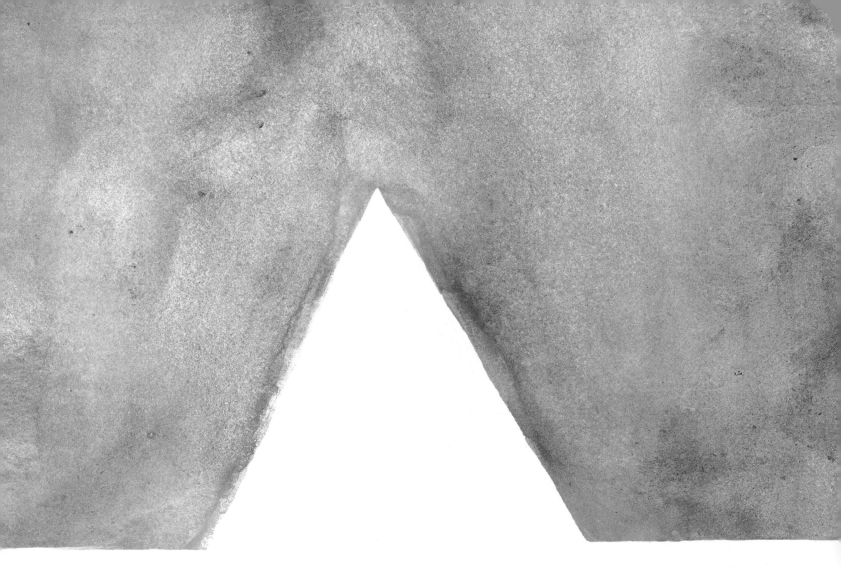

And that is Triangle's door.

One day Triangle walked out of his door
and away from his house.

He was going to play a sneaky trick on Square.

He walked past small triangles

and medium triangles and big triangles.

He walked past shapes

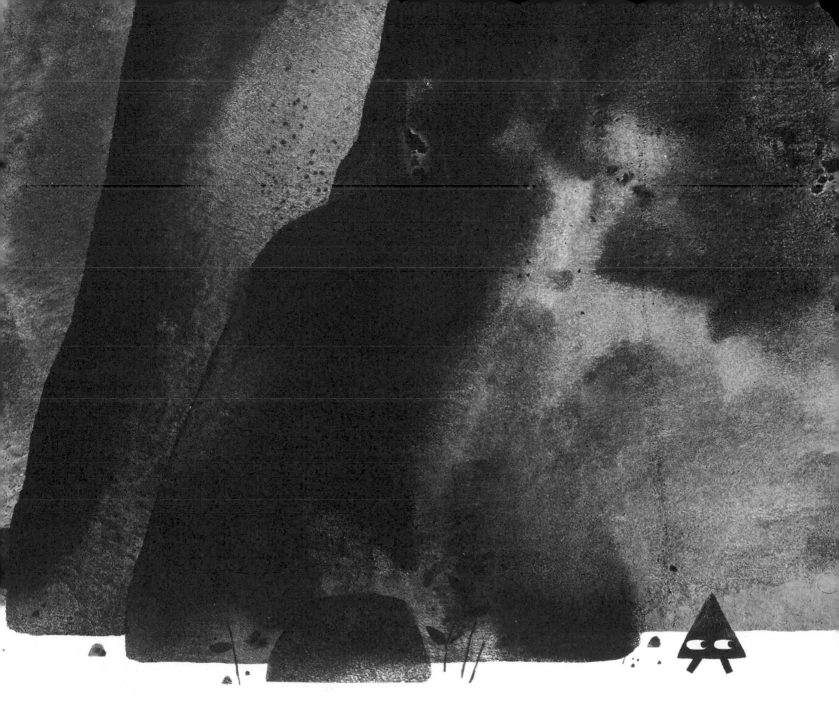

that weren't triangles any more.

They were shapes

with no names.

He walked until he got to a place

where there were squares.

Still thinking of his sneaky trick,
he walked past big squares

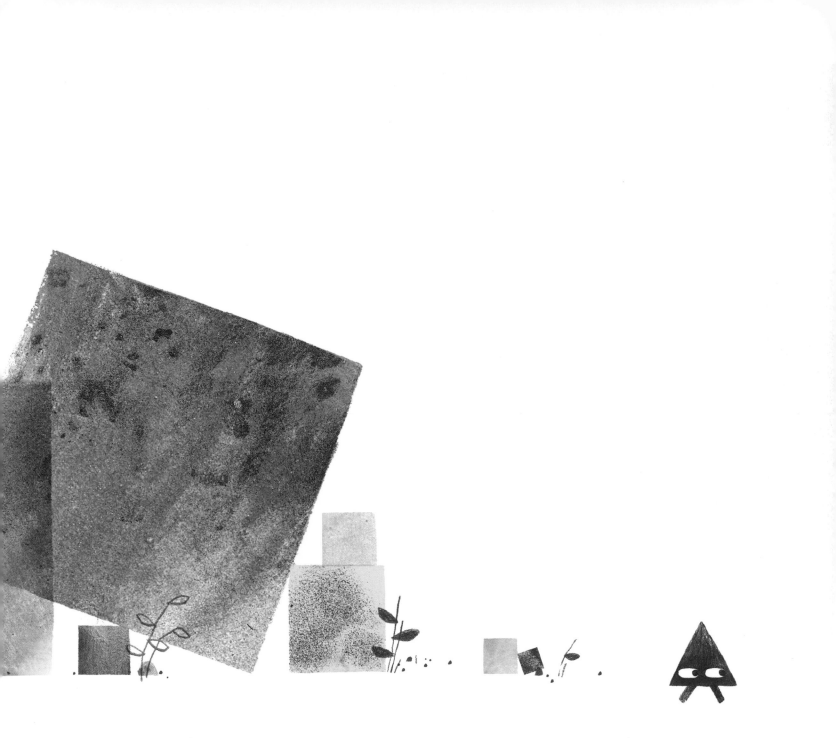

and medium squares and small squares

until he got to Square's house.
"Now," said Triangle,

"I will play my sneaky trick."

Triangle walked up to Square's door

and said "HISS!" just like a snake.

Square was afraid of snakes.

"Oh me oh my!" said Square.

"Go away, you snake! Leave my door!"

"HISS!" said Triangle. "HISS! HISS! HISS!"

"Oh dear dear dear!" said Square.

"How many snakes are out there? Ten?
Ten million? Go away, snakes!"

Triangle could not hiss any more.
He was laughing too hard.

"Triangle!" said Square. "Is that you?"
"Yes!" said Triangle. "I know you are afraid of
snakes. I have played a sneaky trick on you!"

Square ran after Triangle, past small squares

and medium squares and big squares.

He ran past the shapes

with no names,

past the big triangles

and medium triangles and small triangles,

up to Triangle's house and right through his door.

Almost.

"You are stuck!" Triangle laughed and laughed.

Then he stopped. His house was all dark.
Triangle was afraid of the dark.
"It's too dark!" said Triangle. "You're blocking
my light! Go away, you block! Leave my door!"

It was Square's turn to laugh.
"I know you are afraid of the dark. Now I have
played a sneaky trick on you! You see, Triangle,
this was my plan all along."

But do you really believe him?

MAC BARNETT & JON KLASSEN
have made six books together: *Sam and Dave Dig a Hole,*
Extra Yarn, The Wolf, the Duck and the Mouse, Square,
Circle and *Triangle,* which is the book you are reading
right now. Jon is also the creator of the much-acclaimed
Hat trilogy, which includes *I Want My Hat Back,* the Kate
Greenaway and Caldecott Medal winner *This Is Not My
Hat* and *We Found a Hat.* They both live in California,
USA, but in different cities. Jon's Canadian; Mac's not.

Look out for SQUARE and CIRCLE: